I Scream, You Scream

I Scream, You Scream

A FEAST OF FOOD RHYMES

Lillian Morrison

Illustrations by Nancy Dunaway

August House LittleFolk

Printed in the United States of America
10 9 8 7 6 5 4 3 2 1   HB

LIBRARY OF CONGRESS CATALOGING-IN-PUBLICATION DATA
Morrison, Lillian.
I scream, you scream : a feast of food rhymes / Lillian Morrison ; illustrations by Nancy Dunaway.
    p.   cm.
Includes bibliographical references (p. 95).
Summary: a collection of traditional rhymes, chants, taunts, autograph album rhymes, valentines, street cries, and jingles about food.
ISBN 0-87483-495-3 (acid-free paper)
1. Food—Juvenile poetry. 2. Children's poetry, American. [1. Food—Poetry. 2. American poetry—Collections.] I. Dunaway, Nancy, 1947–   ill. II. Title.
PS3563.08747I16   1997
811'.54—dc21   97-19796

To Emma for her culinary interests and her friendship

L. M.

For Mable with love

N.L.D.

Preface

One of the earliest chants I remember hearing as a child growing up in Jersey City, New Jersey, was "I scream, you scream, we all scream for ice cream!" That little rhyme with its sound, rhythm, and pun pleased me immensely. And, of course, as kids we all loved ice cream.

We like some foods and others we don't. Some foods are good for us (not always the ones we like) and some are not. But everybody needs to eat to stay alive. And there are various rules of etiquette about eating that we learn along the way.

Over the years, ordinary people whose names we don't know, children and grown ups alike, have made up verses and sayings about such matters as food and eating—to teach, to tease, to mock, to express love, to jump rope to, or just for fun. Even the peddlers who sold food on the street in the old days yelled catchy verses to entice buyers.

In this book, I have put together a selection of these folk rhymes and sayings—chants, taunts, autograph album rhymes, snatches of folk song, valentines, street cries, and other miscellaneous jingles. Most are American, gathered from friends and acquaintances, my own memory, and from other collectors, with a few rhymes from Mother Goose thrown in. Some are wise; some are just silly or amusing. In any case, they are here for you to enjoy, so:

> Take a bit, take a bite.
> It's good for your appetite.

Lillian Morrison

Contents

Come to My Party!

Come to my party,

Don't be late;

Eat all you want,

But don't eat the plate.

Hot boiled beans and very good butter,
Ladies and gentlemen come to supper.

Wake up, Jacob, day's a breakin';
Pease in the pot and hoecake bakin'.

Get out of bed, sleepyhead;
Get up, you lazy sinner;
We need the sheets for the tablecloth
And it's nearly time for dinner.

When you are married

And your husband is cross,

Come over to my house

And have some applesauce.

Polly put the kettle on,
Polly put the kettle on,
Polly put the kettle on,
We'll all have tea.

Sukey take it off again,
Sukey take it off again,
Sukey take it off again,
They've all gone away.

Blow the fire and make the toast,
Put the muffins down to roast,
Blow the fire and make the toast,
We'll all have tea.

There was a young man so benighted,
He never knew when he was slighted.
He went to a party
And ate just as hearty
As if he'd been really invited.

Whoo! Whoo!

Who cooks for you-all?

Whoo! Whoo!

Who cooks for you-all?

My sister Sue boils the stew;

Who cooks for you-all?

Get Your Elbows off the Table

Mabel, Mabel, strong and able,

Get your elbows off the table.

This is not a horse's stable.

When they pass the pink ice cream
Don't act as if you'd like to scream.
Just turn your head the other way—
Act like you had it every day.

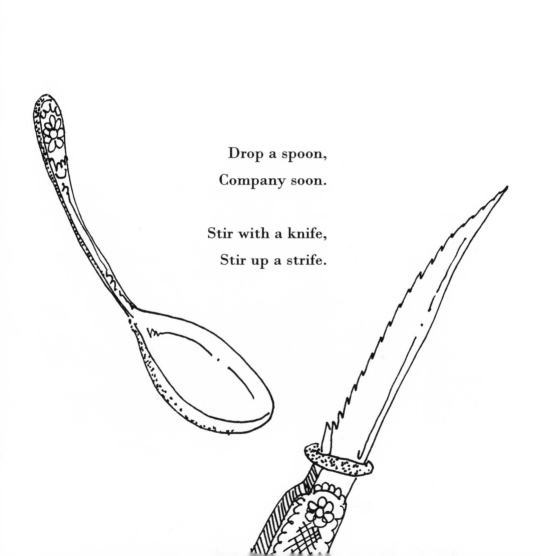

Drop a spoon,
Company soon.

Stir with a knife,
Stir up a strife.

Through the teeth,
Past the gums;
Look out, stomach,
Here it comes!

Sing a song of sixpence,
A pocket full of rye;
Don't you eat that grapefruit
And squirt it in my eye!

Yes, Ma'am, no, Ma'am,
Thank you, Ma'am, please;
Open up the chicken
And fork out the peas.

If you will munch a sprig of parsley,
You needn't eat your onions sparsely.

If you eat crumbs, it will make you wise.
If you leave the crust, you're sure to bust.

An Apple a Day

An apple a day
Keeps the doctor away.

Eat an apple before going to bed,
Make the doctor beg his bread.

Don't tell your friends about your indigestion.

"How are you?" is a greeting, not a question.

Old Aunt Dinah sick in the bed
Called for the doctor;
The doctor said,
"All you need's some short'nin' bread."

Raspberry, strawberry, cherry pie,

You love them all and so do I.

I would reduce
But what's the use?
The bigger the berry
The sweeter the juice.

Mary had a little lamb,
A lobster and some prunes,
A glass of milk, a piece of pie,
And then some macaroons.

It made the busy waiters grin
To see her order so,
And when they carried Mary out
Her face was white as snow.

Beans and potatoes

Are good for soup.

They make your belly

Go l^{o}o$_p$-t$_e$^{e}-l^o^{o}p.

X, Y, Z,
Sugar on your bread,
Cereal in the morning,
And cocoa going to bed.

Tomatoes, lettuce, carrots, peas,
Mother said you've got to eat a lot of these.

Where are you going, Bob?

Down the street, Bob.

For what, Bob?

For rhu-bob.

Let's go, Bob.

No, Bob.

Why, Bob?

Because I don't like rhu-bob.

They say that in the navy
The biscuits are so fine.
But one dropped off the table
And killed a pal of mine.

They say that in the navy
The chicken is so fine.
A leg dropped off the table
And started marking time.

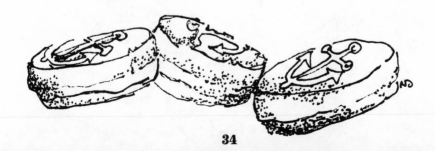

I scream,

You scream,

We all scream

For ice cream!

Do You Carrot All for Me?

Do you carrot all for me?

My heart beets for you,

With your turnip nose

And your radish face,

You are a peach.

If we cantaloupe,

Lettuce marry;

Weed make a swell pear.

I love coffee,

I love tea.

How many boys

Are stuck on me?

Johnny gave me apples.
Johnny gave me pears.
Johnny gave me fifty cents
And kissed me on the stairs.

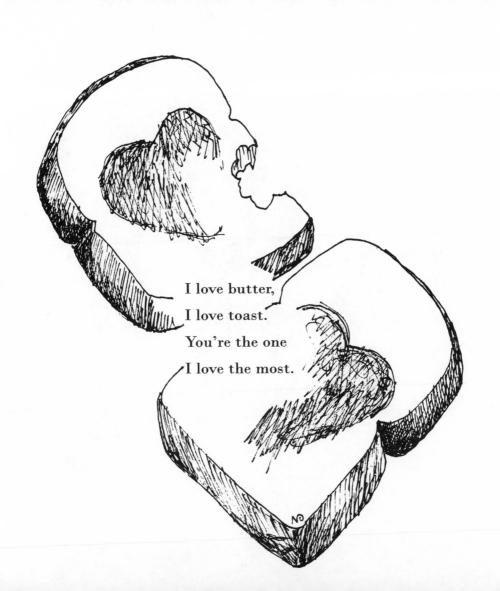

I love butter,
I love toast.
You're the one
I love the most.

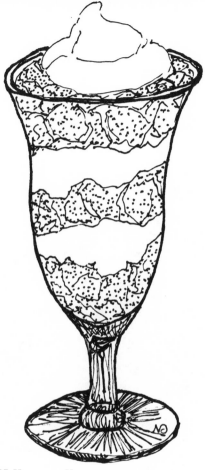

Yellow, yellow,

                Kiss your fellow;

Go upstairs and

                Eat some jello.

Sugar is sugar
And salt is salt.

If you don't love me,
It's sure your own fault.

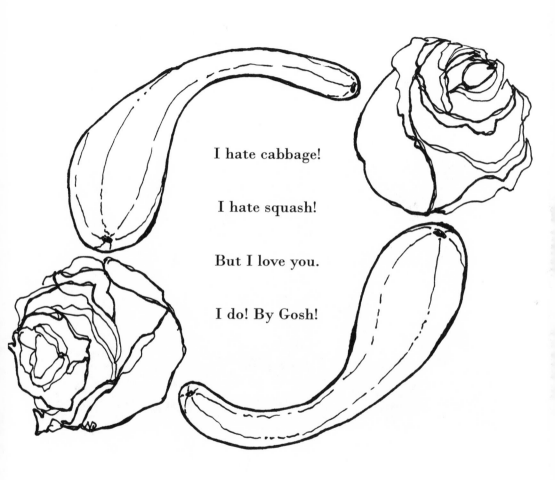

I hate cabbage!

I hate squash!

But I love you.

I do! By Gosh!

I love my wife.

I love my baby.

I love my biscuits

Sopped in gravy.

Yours till the milk shakes.

Yours till jelly rolls.

Yours till potatoes wear specs for sore eyes.

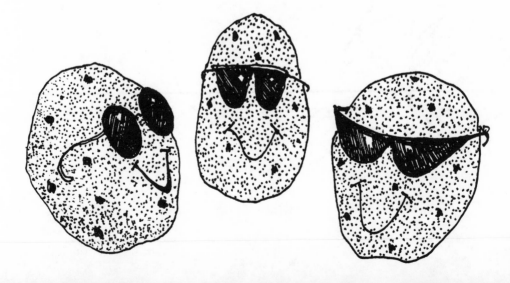

May your husband be like a chocolate ice cream soda—

Tall, dark, and luscious.

I love peaches.

I love pie.

I love a little girl

About so high.

Ice cream soda, lemonade punch,
Tell me the initial of my honeybunch.

Roses are red
Violets are blue
Garlic is strong
And I'm garlic for you.

If All the World Was an Apple Pie

If all the world was an apple pie
And all the sea was ink
And all the trees were bread and cheese
What should we have for drink?

No matter how young a prune may be

It's always full of wrinkles.

A baby prune is like its dad

But doesn't have wrinkles very bad.

We've got wrinkles on our face.

A prune's got wrinkles every place.

You can lead a guitar to water

but

You can't tuna fish.

As I was walking by the lake,
I met a little rattlesnake.
I gave him so much jelly cake
It made his little belly ache.

Knock, knock.
Who's there?
Banana.
Banana who?

Knock, knock.
Who's there?
Banana.
Banana who?

Knock, knock.
Who's there?
Banana.
Banana who?

Knock, knock.
Who's there?
Orange.
Orange who?

Orange you glad I didn't say banana?

I wish I were a fly,

I'd buzz about all day

And eat molasses candy

Without a cent to pay.

Johnny's too little to whittle,
Give him some blueberry jam;
Take off his bib, put him into his crib,
And feed him on doughnuts and ham.

Good king Wenceslas walked out
In his mother's garden,
Bumped into a brussels sprout
And said, "I beg your pardon."

Run, chicken, run,
The farmer's got a gun;
His wife has got the oven hot
And you're the One.

Trick or treat,
Smell my feet,
Give me something
Good to eat.

1, 2, 3, a-larie,

    I spy Auntie Mary

        Coming out of David's Dairy

            Eating chocolate ice cream.

On Top of Spaghetti

(To be sung to the tune of "On Top of Old Smoky")

On top of spaghetti, all covered with cheese,
I lost my poor meatball 'cause I had to sneeze.
It rolled off the table and onto the floor,
And then my poor meatball went out of the door.
It went in the garden and under a bush,
And then my poor meatball was nothing but mush.
So if you have spaghetti, all covered with cheese,
Hold on to your meatball and try not to sneeze.

On Nevski Bridge a Russian stood
Chewing his beard for lack of food.
Said he, "It's tough this stuff to eat
But a darn sight better than shredded wheat!"

Humpty Dumpty sat on a wall.

Humpty Dumpty had a great f

                                                a

                                                        l

                                                            l.

All the king's horses and all the king's men

Had s^cr_am_b^l_ed eggs.

I'm Popeye the sailor man;
I live in a garbage can;
I eat all the worms
And spit out the germs,
I'm Popeye the sailor man.

"I was always religiously inclined,"
Said the oyster as he slid down
The minister's throat, "but never
Did I dream I'd enter the clergy."

How many cookies could a good cook cook

If a good cook could cook cookies?

As many cookies as a good cook could cook

If a good cook could cook cookies.

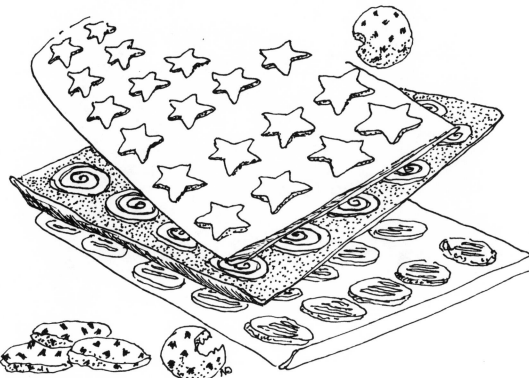

You Tell 'Em, Pie Face

What's cookin', good lookin'?
Whatchu mean, jelly bean?
Don't give me no lip, potato chip.
Shut up, ketchup.
I'm the boss, applesauce.
It's your fault, garlic salt.

Which hand do you eat with?

My right.

You dirty kid.

Why don't you use a spoon?

You tell 'em, Pie Face,

You've got the crust.

Do you have chicken legs?

Yes, we do.

Well, wear long pants

And they won't show.

How do you like your carrots?
Raw! Raw! Raw!
How do you like your cabbage!
Slaw! Slaw! Slaw!
How do you like your chocolate?
Sweet! Sweet! Sweet!
How do you like Woodrow High?
Tweet! Tweet! Tweet!
They're for the birds.

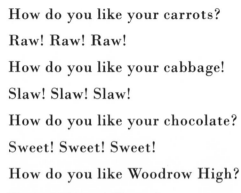

Roses are red,
Violets are blue.
Cabbage stinks,
And so do you.

Be like a banana and split.

Root Beer, Sold Here

Root Beer,
Sold Here.

Sign in a delicatessen window:

Send a salami
To your boy in the army.

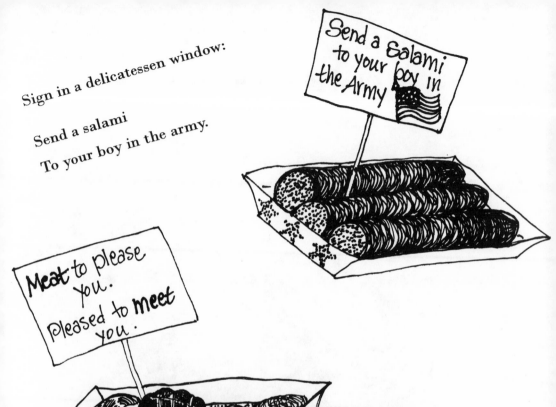

Sign in a butcher shop:

Meat to please you.
Pleased to meet you.

Ice-cold Lemonade!
Freeze your teeth, curl your hair,
Make you feel like a millionaire!

Here's your ice-cold lemonade!
It's made in the shade
And stirred with a spade.
Come buy my ice-cold lemonade!

It's made in the shade
And sold in the sun.
If you ain't got no money,
You can't git none.

One glass for a nickel
And two for a dime.
If you ain't got the change,
You can't git mine.

I got artichokes by the neck!

Plums, ripe plums!
B I G as your thumbs!

Shad Song

I got shad.
Ain't you glad?
I got shad
So don't get mad.
I got shad.
Go tell your dad.
It's the best old shad
He ever had.
I got shad.
Caught 'em in the sun.
I got shad.
I caught 'em just for fun.
So if you ain't got no money,
You can't get none.
I got shad.
Ain't you glad?
I got shad.
Tell your great-grandad.
It's the best old shad
He ever had.

Clams to sell! Fine clams today!
Clams nice and soft from Rockaway!
Clams to bake and clams to fry
And clams to make a clam potpie.
Oh clams!

        Oh clams!

                Soft clams!

Tell your dads and tell your mams
That I'm the boy to sell 'em clams.

Watermelons, come and see-ee.

   Every one sold on a guarantee!

Red ripe watermelons! Sweet and juicy,

   Fit for you and fit for Lucy!

The world goes around
And the sun comes down
And I got the best
Hot Tamales in town!

Taste and try
Before you buy.

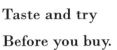

I says, you says,
We all want ices.

Peter's pop kept a lollipop shop,
And the lollipop shop kept Peter.

A cup of coffee in a copper coffee cup.

Eat fresh fried fish free at the fish fry.

Betty bit a bite of butter, but the bite of butter
Betty bit was a bitter bite of butter.

I bought a box of biscuits, a box of mixed biscuits,
and a biscuit mixer.

Peter Piper picked a peck of pickled peppers,
A peck of pickled peppers Peter Piper picked.
If Peter Piper picked a peck of pickled peppers,
Where's the peck of pickled peppers Peter Piper picked?

There was a young fellow named Tate

Who dined with a friend at 8:08.

But I hate to relate

What this person named Tate

And his tête-à-tête ate at 8:08.

Bless the Bread, Bless the Meat

Bless the meat,

Forget the skin.

Open your mouth

And cram it in.

Heavenly Father, bless us,
And keep us all alive;
There's ten of us for dinner
And not enough for five.

One word's as good as ten.

Fall to, and

Amen.

Good Lord, make us able

To eat all on the table.

If there's more in the pot,

Let's get it while it's hot.

Morning is here,
The board is spread,
Thanks be to God
Who gives us bread.

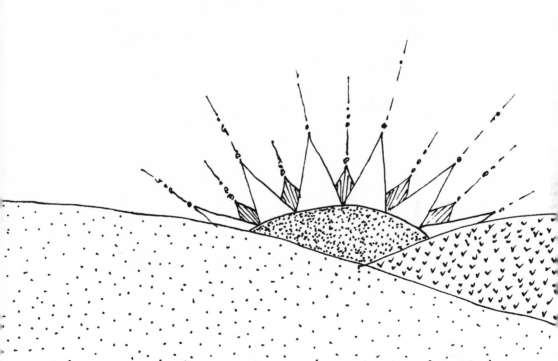

Bless the bread.

Bless the meat.

It's getting late.

Let's eat.

Before listing printed sources, I wish to thank the following people who gave me rhymes, information leading to rhymes, or lent me useful material. Since I have been gathering folk rhymes for almost fifty years, it is not surprising that a number of these contributors are no longer living. My thanks to Martha Cooper, Delia Davis, Aline Grant, Philomena Casella Houlihan, Sally-Ruth Isenburg, Theresa Cassella Ivanier, Robert Koeppl, Carol McCurdy, Eve Merriam, Daniel Morrison, William Eliot Morrison, Suzi Parker, Mary Read, Eileen Riols, Doris Ritzman, and Jane Ross. Thanks, too, to Dr. Elizabeth Pilant and to Carol Moser for several rhymes from their mimeographed collections of American folk rhymes made under the auspices of the National Conference American Folklore for Youth, Ball State Teachers College, Muncie, Indiana. I am especially indebted as well to the folklorists and the fellow collectors listed below and to The New York Public Library whose vast resources have supplied me with most of my printed source material.

Abrahams, Roger D. *Jump-Rope Rhymes: A Dictionary*. Austin, Texas: University of Texas Press, 1969.

Agee, Hugh. "Good Bread, Good Meat: Folk Blessings in the English Class." *English Journal*, V.70, No. 6, 1981.

Bergen, Fanny D. *Current Superstitions Collected from the Oral Tradition of English Speaking Folk*. Boston: Houghton, 1896.

Botkin, B.A. *Sidewalks of America*. Indianapolis, Indiana: Bobbs Merrill, 1954.

Brady, Ellis. *All in ! All in! A Selection of Dublin Children's Traditional Street Games*. Dublin: Comhairle Bhéaloideas, 1975.

Brand, Oscar. *The Ballad Mongers*. Westport, Conn.: Greenwood, 1979.

Brewster, Paul G. "Children's Games and Rhymes" in *The Frank C. Brown Collection of North Carolina Folklore*, V. 1. Durham, North Carolina: Duke University Press, 1952.

Brockway, Walter, and B.K. Winer. *Homespun America*. New York: Simon and Schuster, 1958.

Browne, Ray. "Parodied Prayers and Scripture." *Journal of American Folklore*, V. 72, No. 283, 1959.

Coffin, Peter Tristram, and Henry Cohen. *Folklore from the Working Folk of America*. Garden City, New York: Doubleday, 1973.

Cole, William. *Poem Stew*. New York: Harper, 1981

de Angeli, Marguerite. *Book of Nursery and Mother Goose Rhymes*. Garden City, New York: Doubleday, 1954

Dorson, Richard M. *American Folklore*. Chicago: University of Chicago Press, 1959.

Emrich, Duncan. *Folklore on the American Land*. Boston: Little, Brown, 1972.

_____ . *The Hodgepodge Book*. New York: Four Winds, 1972.

_____. *The Nonsense Book*. New York: Four Winds, 1970.

Esar, Evan. *The Humor of Humor*. New York: Horizon. 1952.

Falk, Bonnie Hughes. *Forget-Me-Not: A Collection of Autograph Verses, 1880s-1980s*. Stillwater, Minn.: Croixside Press, 1984.

Haan, Marina H., and R.B. Hammerstrom. *Graffiti in the Southwest Conference*. New York: Warner, 1981.

Harder, Kelsie B. "Jingle Lore of Pigtails, Pals, and Puppy Love." *Tennessee Folklore Society Bulletin*, V. 22, 1956.

_____. *A Selection of Youngstown, Ohio Autograph Verses*. Chillicothe, Ohio: Ohio Valley Folk Publications, New Series, No. 73, 1961.

Hindley, Charles. *A History of the Cries of London*. London, 1884. Reissue Detroit: Singing Tree Press, 1969.

Johnson, Clifton. *What They Say in New England...* Boston: Lee & Shepard, 1897.

Kelen, Emery. *Proverbs of Many Nations*. New York: Lothrop, Lee & Shepard, 1966.

Knapp, Mary, and Herbert Knapp. *One Potato, Two Potato...* New York: W.W. Norton, 1976.

Koken, John M. *Here's to It! Toasts for All Occasions*. New York: A.S. Barnes, 1960.

Livingston, Myra Cohn. *Lots of Limericks*. New York: Margaret K. McElderry Books, 1991.

Mook, Maurice A. "Tongue Tanglers from Central Pennsylvania." *Journal of American Folklore*, V. 72, No. 286, 1959.

Opie, Iona, and Peter Opie. *I Saw Esau*. London: Williams & Norgate, 1947.

_____. *The Oxford Dictionary of Nursery Rhymes*. Oxford: Oxford University Press, 1951.

_____. *The Lore and Language of Schoolchildren*. Oxford: Oxford University Press, 1959.

Prelutsky, Jack. *Poems of A. Nonny Mouse*. New York: Knopf, 1989.

Randolph, Vance. *Ozark Folk Songs*. Columbia, Missouri: The State Historical Society of Missouri, 1949.

Ripley, Elizabeth. *Nothing but Nonsense*. New York: Farrar & Rinehart, 1943.

Saxon, Lyle, et al. *Gumbo Ya-Ya*. Gretna, Louisiana: Pelican Publishing Co., 1986.

Silcock, Arnold. *Verse and Worse*. London: Faber & Faber, 1942.

Talley, Thomas W. *Negro Folk Rhymes: Wise and Otherwise*. New York: Macmillan, 1922.

Tidwell, James N. *A Treasury of American Folk Humor*. New York: Crown, 1956.

Withers, Carl. *A Rocket in My Pocket*. New York: Holt, 1948.

Wood, Ray. *Fun in American Folk Rhymes*. Philadelphia: Lippincott, 1952.

Date Due

APR 1 5 1999				